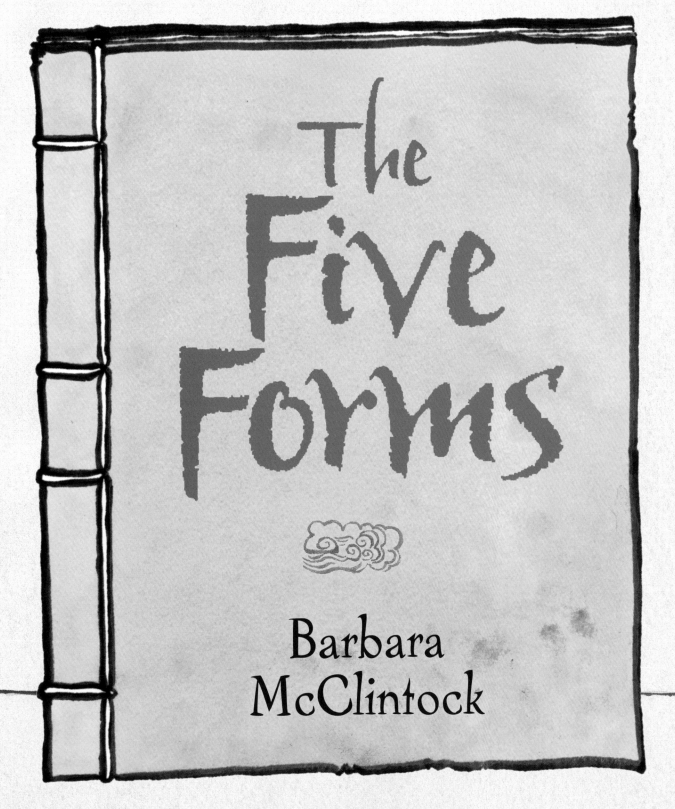

The Five Forms

Barbara McClintock

FARRAR STRAUS GIROUX

New York

In the ancient Chinese tradition of martial arts, there are movements called forms. Some forms mimic the postures and temperaments of animals. When practiced correctly, these forms release the power of the animals they represent. However, if the forms are performed by anyone other than a master, there could be unexpected results.

These forms look pretty easy to do.

Do not attempt these forms without an experienced teacher!

The second form is
LEOPARD.
Leopard overpowers
Crane.

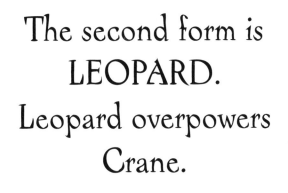

The fourth is DRAGON.
Dragon overpowers
Snake.

The final form returns everything
to the way it was.
It is to be performed only
by a Grand Master!

Surprise!

My son, Larson DiFiori, has been studying and practicing martial arts (wushu) since he was fourteen. After college, he studied at a martial arts academy in Xi'an, China, for a year, and briefly at the Wudang Daoist Traditional Kung Fu Academy in Hubei province. In 2009, Larson won two gold medals for sword form at the Hong Kong International Wushu Championship. He is currently a doctoral candidate in East Asian religious traditions at Brown University, and he continues to study and practice qigong, kung fu, and other forms of wushu.

Larson was my inspiration for *The Five Forms*, as well as my adviser, research assistant, and fact-and form-checker as I worked on the book. Fortunately, he has never brought any animals to life as the direct result of his martial-arts practice.

This book is for him.

Farrar Straus Giroux Books for Young Readers
An imprint of Macmillan Publishing Group, LLC
175 Fifth Avenue, New York, NY 10010

Text and illustrations copyright © 2017 by Barbara McClintock
All rights reserved
Color separations by Bright Arts (H.K.) Ltd.
Printed in China by RR Donnelley Asia Printing Solutions Ltd.,
Dongguan City, Guangdong Province
Designed by Roberta Pressel
First edition, 2017
1 3 5 7 9 10 8 6 4 2

mackids.com

Library of Congress Control Number: 2016057826
ISBN: 978-1-62672-216-3